Enjoy the quiet moments

Christie Sverrig

Flutterby, My Butterfly

Written by Christie Tierney

Illustrated by Chloë Grass

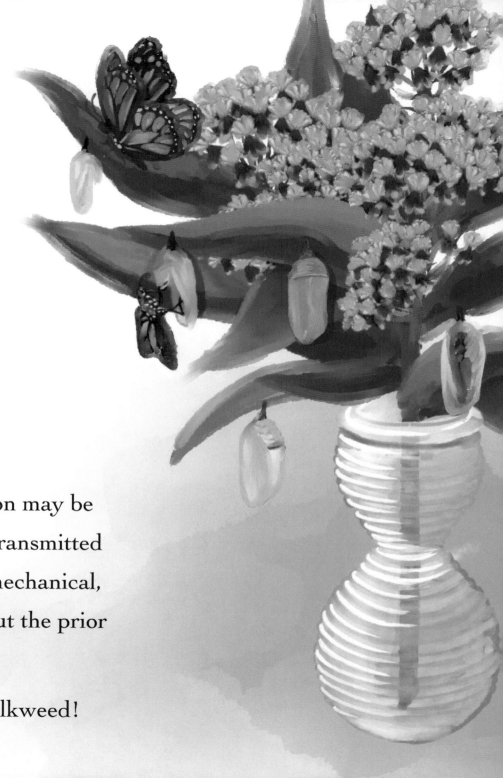

Co-Published by Freeze Time Media and Milkweed!

To my husband, Pat, who knew I was a writer long before I ever did. He is a man who works tirelessly to ensure our boys enjoy every opportunity possible. I am especially grateful for the time I was given to be at home with our sons when they were young, and unbeknownst to me, to live a "storybook" life I would later write about.

Early one bright summer morning, three little boys woke up knowing the day they had been waiting for had arrived!

It was caterpillar season! There was a very special glass box on the counter in their kitchen where every day, magical things would happen! Today was the day they would fill that glass box.

"Can we go now, Mom?" asked James.

"Please, please!" cried Ryan and Jack.

"Yes, grab your shoes and let's go! C'mon, Rookie," she said to their dog as he wagged his tail with excitement.

The three boys headed out with their mom, excited to see who would find the first milkweed plant with a caterpillar egg on it!

Just as everyone was searching, a monarch butterfly fluttered by. Little Jack pointed up at the sky and exclaimed, "A flutterby!"

The two older boys laughed and laughed.

"Remember," said Mom, "When a butterfly flutters by. …"

"We know, Mom," said Ryan, "be still, listen, and tell me what you're thinking."

"My tummy is rumbling for lunch!" said James.

"Do monarch butterflies always lay their eggs on milkweed leaves?" asked Ryan.

"We love you, Mommy," said Jack.

L ater that morning, they placed the first bouquet of milkweed along with teeny, tiny monarch caterpillar eggs into the magical glass box.

Each day, they watched for the very moment a baby caterpillar would hatch. They took many walks to hunt for fresh milkweed because those caterpillars ate and ate and grew and grew.

Eventually, each caterpillar spun a beautiful chrysalis sealed with golden thread. They watched closely and waited, because before long, inside that magical glass box, a beautiful monarch butterfly would emerge.

O nce the butterfly's wings were ready, this meant one thing.

They got to take it outside and release it into the sunshine.

And as always, as each monarch fluttered off, their mom would say,

"When a butterfly flutters by,

be still, listen, and tell me what you're thinking."

"I love flutterbys SO much!" smiled Jack.

"Off to the sunshine and flowers, little friend," said James.

"I think this little guy loves me and wants to stay," said Ryan.

Late the next summer, the boys were outside playing in the sandbox when a monarch quietly landed right on Ryan's arm!

"Shhhhh. Be still, listen, and tell us what you're thinking," whispered Jack.

"I'm nervous about starting kindergarten," said Ryan. "I'm the first and I have to go all by myself."

"But Ryan," said James, "remember, when you are there, be still, and listen, and when you come home, you can tell us what you're thinking!"

Ryan smiled and the butterfly fluttered away.

One day, when the boys were a bit older, they spent the afternoon with their little cousin at Grandma Cookie's house. As they were driving home, James said excitedly, "Mom, did you know that Grandma Cookie lived in the city and walked to school every day when she was little? Even in the winter! And after school, she played in the building's elevator with her cousin! They went up and down, and up and down."

"How in the world do you know this?" Mom asked.

"Because when we were helping Grandma in her garden, a butterfly fluttered by and we said, "Be still, Grandma, listen, and tell us what you're thinking! And she did!"

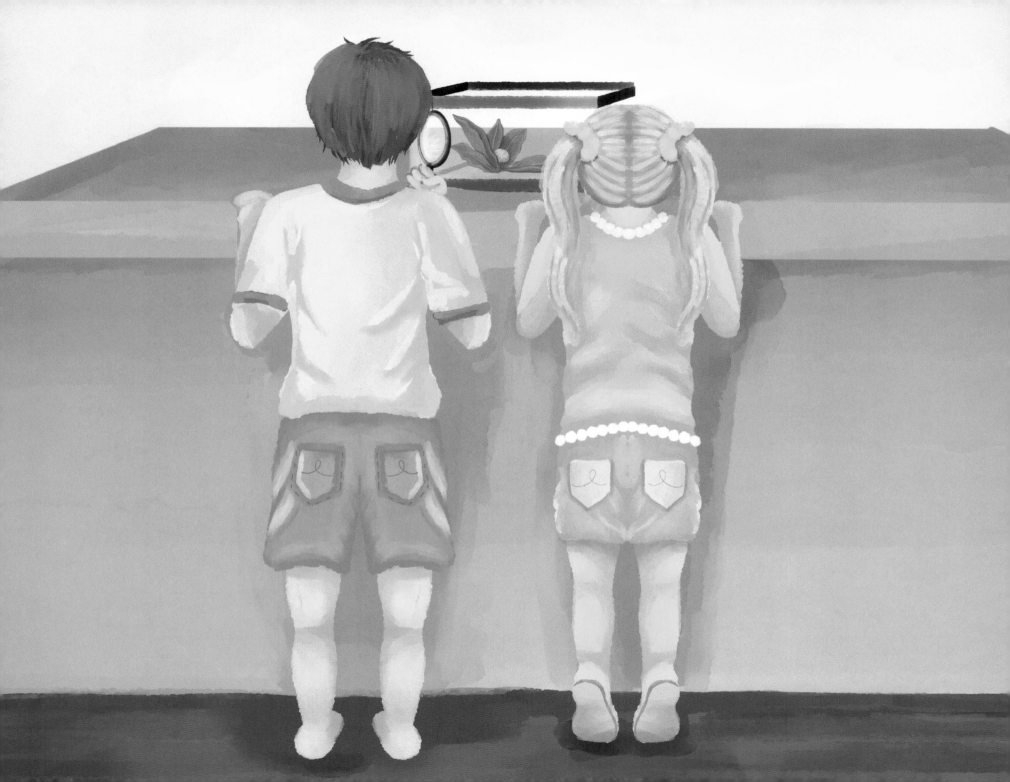

Throughout the years, the boys enjoyed teaching friends how to find the special caterpillar eggs, and soon they too had beautiful monarch butterflies hatching in their kitchens.

The boys grew and grew, just like the little caterpillars. Every summer, even after those little boys grew up, their mom still took those walks, and she couldn't walk past a milkweed plant without hunting for those tiny caterpillar eggs.

S he treasured those quiet summer
  moments with her little boys, and as
she did, she thought fondly to herself,

"Flutterby, my butterflies,

but as you grow, please always know,

far or near, I'm always here.

Remember to be still, listen, and tell me
what you're thinking."

Raising Monarch Butterflies is EASY!

Milkweed (Asclepias) is the ONLY plant monarch butterflies will lay their eggs on and is the ONLY plant monarch caterpillars will eat. Common milkweed grows naturally along walking paths, near the edges of ponds, in prairies, and along roadsides. When you spot a plant, search for eggs or caterpillars near the top of the plant on the underside of the leaf. Female monarchs typically lay one egg per milkweed plant. Eggs are off-white or yellow, characterized by longitudinal ridges that run from the pointed tip to the base, and are about the size of a pencil tip or a period on a page but big enough to see. Once you find something, snip that part of the plant, and bring it inside. Put the milkweed in an upright flower tube or small mouthed vase with water and place inside a container with a secure lid that will allow plenty of light and air.

The tip of an egg will turn black about four days after it is laid. This is the head of the tiny caterpillar about to hatch. Always keep fresh milkweed for your hungry caterpillars. You may be surprised at how many new eggs and caterpillars you "accidentally" bring in with your fresh milkweed, so always be on the lookout! Caterpillars will molt four times during their first ten to fourteen days.

Beware! Caterpillars POOP! You may want to line your container with paper towels that can be replaced to keep things clean. Eventually, full-grown caterpillars leave the milkweed plant to search for a place to form their chrysalis. It will settle quietly and then hang like a "J." When the "J" starts to wiggle, you will see it molt one last time to reveal its beautiful chrysalis.

For the next nine to fourteen days, a magical transformation happens inside the chrysalis. Watch for it to turn milky and then black. When it turns black, look closely and you will be able to see the orange and black of the monarch's wings. At this point, things happen rather quickly. The chrysalis will crack, and the monarch will emerge with tiny, crumpled, wet wings. It will cling to the chrysalis shell as it pumps hemolymph through its body and wings. After about an hour, the wings will be full sized, dry, and fluttering. Take your container outside, reach inside, and let the monarch crawl onto your finger, taking care not to touch the wings. Let it crawl until it flies away or place it on a flower or bush. If your monarch has a single black dot on each wing, it is a male.

In this chaotic, hustle and bustle world, my message to "be still, listen, and tell me what you're thinking" is intended to help us all slow down, be present with one another, and enjoy the quiet moments.

For more information on all things milkweed, caterpillars and monarchs, visit www.milkweedonline.com

About the Author

Christie Tierney was a young stay-at-home mom of three boys when a neighbor introduced them to the joy of raising monarch butterflies. Twenty years later, she continues to pass along this treasured summer tradition.

A hockey mom of three, Christie loves outdoor adventure, constant activity, and entertaining friends at their family lake house. She is an avid monarch butterfly and milkweed enthusiast and takes every opportunity to educate others about the preservation and cultivation of pollinator habitats!

Now that the boys are grown, Christie and her husband, Pat, enjoy long walks during the summer with their dog, Rookie. To this day, she cannot walk past a milkweed plant without searching for those caterpillars!

About the Illustrator

Chloë Grass is an artist with a portfolio including all types of mediums such as painting, illustrating, and sculpting. She has had a great passion for all forms of art since a very young age and continues to challenge herself to grow her artistic abilities. She is currently studying at Arts University Bournemouth where she is majoring in Makeup for Media and Performance. In the future she plans to work as a prosthetic makeup artist for film and television while continuing to illustrate.

CPSIA information can be obtained at www.ICGtesting.com
Printed in the USA
LVIW012047250321
682527LV00001B/3